D1544631

THE 24 ELVES OF CHRISTMAS

Meet the North Pole Council

Created by
ROB SUTHERLAND

Written by
RACHEL CATHEY

Illustrated by
JACQUI DAVIS AND JOSIAH HENDRICKSON

- BEAVER'S POND PRESS -

MINNEAPOLIS, MN

Edited by Hanna Kjeldbjerg
Illustrated by Jacqui Davis and Josiah Hendrickson
Production editor: Hanna Kjeldbjerg

ISBN 13: 978-1-59298-735-1
Library of Congress Catalog Number: 2019904673
Printed in the United States of America
First Printing: 2020
24 23 22 21 20   5 4 3 2 1

Book design and typesetting by Dan Pitts.

7108 Ohms Lane
Edina, MN 55439-2129
(952) 829-8818
www.BeaversPondPress.com

To order, visit www.24elves.com. Reseller discounts available.

Contact Rob Sutherland at www.24elves.com for school visits, speaking engagements, freelance writing projects, and interviews.

THIS BOOK IS DEDICATED TO:

Will, Ella, and Matthew who are my inspiration and make me
a better person. They have helped me make the magic of Christmas.

My mom who reminds me to see the good and work through everything
with a positive attitude and kindness.

Rachel, Jacqui, and Josiah who have brought this vision to life.

All my family and friends who have encouraged, supported,
and believed in this project.

-RS

A NOTE FROM SANTA

Many have called me a jolly elf, and there could not be a better description. I'm Santa Claus. I sometimes go by Old Saint Nick, but my favorite nickname is Father Christmas. I feel like the father of the season of joy, and who wouldn't be jolly while spreading the magic of Christmas around the world?

Everyone knows that my reindeer and I travel to deliver gifts every Christmas Eve. But I'll let you in on a little secret... that's just one night every year. The other 364 days, the other residents of the North Pole are the real heroes of spreading cheer. There's a whole community of elves and it's their job to help everyone remember that thinking of others will, in turn, fill you with joy.

You see, there's so much more to the Christmas season than presents. It's a time for delicious treats, joyous festivals, shimmering lights, remembering family, generous giving, and so much more.

To accomplish all this, Mrs. Claus and I need quite a bit of help. So, a very special council was formed to create, maintain, and protect the magic of Christmas. Every day this month, I'll introduce you to a member of this inspirational crew so you can learn about all they do to create the Christmas season—and how to help spread it yourself, all year round.

BELINA TINSEL

The first special elf you need to meet is Belina from the North Pole Sweet Shop. She's been our most celebrated baker for 112 years and has been a member of the council for ninety-three years. We elves live long lives, and Belina is 632 years young.

It's no surprise that Belina smells of cinnamon since she so frequently uses the delicious spice in her shop. Her favorite treats to bake are cinnamon rolls—she even has her own special recipe! There's always a plate of piping hot cinnamon rolls waiting for me on Christmas when I return from delivering all the toys.

To recognize Belina's generous spirit, I have a special snowman figurine designed every year for her birthday.

Belina has no children of her own, but she's like a grandmother to all the elves. They love to visit her and hear stories about each snowman figurine in her huge collection. They're usually also hoping to be treated to a snack of Smooches or Crystal Delights, some of Granny Tinsel's sweetest inventions.

When Belina isn't hosting visitors at her home, she likes to fill baskets with sweet treats for winter picnics with her friends. Sometimes she even goes snowshoeing out to her favorite spots.

While she loves all the merriment with her fellow elves, Belina also works tremendously hard. She's the first to arrive at the bakery every morning and the last to leave. Young bakers are fortunate to learn from her at the Sweet Shop, and she frequently mentors new bakers through challenges like the annual North Pole baking contest. Council members are also lucky because she always brings something scrumptious to enjoy at meetings, like caramels, gingersnap cookies, or peanut brittle. Belina helps us all remember that cooking together and sharing good food make us a strong family.

MERTIN EVERGREEN

I'm excited to introduce you to Mertin, the master of the North Pole greenhouses. As I'm sure you can imagine, this is an extremely important job because he needs to grow all the fruits and vegetables we eat. Each greenhouse looks like a glass sculpture, but must be as hearty as it is beautiful. The North Pole is always covered in thick blankets of snow, so Mertin must maintain the greenhouse temperatures at just the right level so all the plants grow healthy and strong. That's a huge job since there are thirty greenhouses to care for, all with different needs!

At 224 years old, Mertin is an expert at growing the best plants. The secret to his success, he says, is how much he sings to them! As a member of the Jingle Tones, the North Pole barbershop quartet, Mertin is always warbling away as he works.

Though Mertin works indoors, he also loves to play outdoors. You can find him playing hockey, skating with friends, or tubing on the big slopes. His good friend Belina taught him how to make Smooches, so he's always prepared to take a break by the firepit and warm up with a sweet treat. His love for hockey was inspired by his grandfather Kertin who helped Mertin perfect his awesome slap shot.

Grandfather Kertin also gave Mertin his most prized possession: a gold pocket watch with an engraving of my face on the outside. Inside there are snowflakes between each number, reminding him that every moment in life is just as special as the unique shape of each frozen flake.

For seventy-six years, Mertin has helped the council to understand that life can flourish in unusual places, just like the plants in the greenhouse of the frozen North Pole.

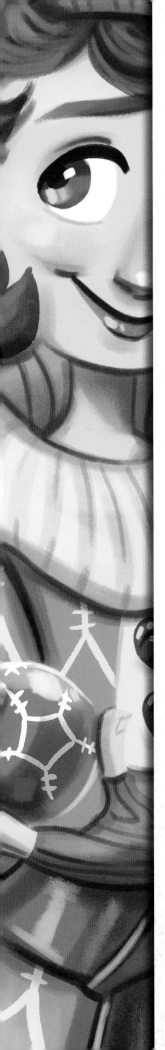

SPARKLES SNOWFLAKE

Today I'd like to introduce you to a very spunky elf named Sparkles. She's my chief ornament designer and creates pieces that bring the sparkle of Christmas to life. Once Sparkles carves and paints a new ornament, a whole team of elves crafts molds so they can make hundreds of copies.

Every year I'm excited to see the ornaments she designs, but her most special creation is always for Mrs. Claus. It is a one-of-a-kind masterpiece that the mother of Christmas hangs on a tree in her piano room.

Now just in case you might think Sparkles is as delicate and fragile as her ornaments, let me tell you—it's not so! When she's not dreaming up ornamental wonders, you'll likely find her at the target range. She's extremely skilled with a snow-bow, and for the past four years she's taken first place in the annual North Pole competition. Our specially designed bows fire off perfectly shaped snowballs that explode with shimmery wonder when they hit their mark. A single snowflake remains to show how many points have been earned.

When not taking aim at targets, Sparkles uses her design skills to decorate cookies. She also volunteers to help decorate for big events and festivals.

At just 225 years old, Sparkles is one of our younger members on the council, but she has been part of the team since she was just forty-two. She helps us see the beauty in the world around us, and her competitive nature reminds us all to keep striving for the best.

DECEMBER 4:

HARVEL BELL

Today I'm here to introduce you to our resident tree farmer and lumberjack, Harvel. I have incredible respect for this hardworking elf who has been on the council for 106 of his 279 years.

Harvel grows trees not only to decorate the North Pole, but also to provide the wood for furniture and, of course, toys! Most of the trees that decorate our little community are magical and grow in special planters so they stay healthy and strong year-round. During the Christmas season, Harvel also scouts out special large evergreens to be cut down to spruce up the place, just like you might do in your home. The day after Thanksgiving, Harvel's team places a gigantic tree in the toy factory to help lift the spirits of the elves, who must work harder than ever to finish all the toys by Christmas Eve.

All year long, Harvel works hard to care for the many types of trees in the tree farm. When they are ready to be harvested, the team cuts them down and loads them onto a sleigh to bring them to the sawmill. There, elves cut them into smaller pieces and send them to toy or furniture workshops.

I have a special chair by the fireplace in my office that was crafted from the dark heartwood of a walnut tree over 150 feet tall! Harvel also collected the savory fruits from that giant tree and gave them to his friend Belina, who baked us many delicious treats that season.

To keep his axe skills sharp, this flannel-clad elf enjoys a bit of friendly competition with Sparkles. His marksmanship with an axe is legendary.

Harvel is always careful to maintain nature's balance by planting new trees to replace those he chops down, reminding the council to find balance in our own daily lives.

SILVIEN IVY

One very important member of our council is the North Pole doctor, Silvien. She is the kindest and most generous elf I know, so it was not a big surprise when she chose her profession.

Much of her time is spent keeping everyone healthy, welcoming new elves into the world, and using a bit of magic to keep serious illnesses out of the North Pole community.

Other elves are always trying to give her presents to thank her for all her good care, but Silvien believes in living a simple life. Rather than take things from others, she prefers to make a beautiful candle and give it to a patient as a comfort while they recover. I still have a candle she gave me a few years back when a nasty Christmas Eve blizzard brought on a bit of the sniffles. It has an acorn and pine needle design and smells of evergreens.

Silvien also has a love (and talent!) for growing flowers. This is why she and Brindle, our master gardener, have become such steadfast friends. Brindle has even given her a special place in one of the greenhouses to grow her flowers. By rotating plants between her home and the greenhouse every season, Silvien always has something fresh and new to enjoy.

Sitting beside her huge, sunny windows, Silvien will gaze out at the birds while she works her magic to arrange a bouquet of cut flowers to give as a special gift to a friend. She has hung up twelve bird feeders and fifteen birdhouses for her feathered friends.

At just 142 years of age, Silvien has learned a lot about looking after elves and nature. It is also important to recognize her as an elf who lives life according to her own rule book, rather than acting a certain way just because others think she should. She helps us all see that it's not the things in life that make us happy, but the care and kindness we show others.

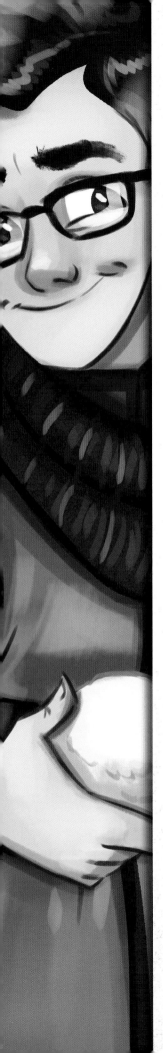

SPINIKER GARLAND

When I have free time, which is rare, you might find me with Spiniker. Spiniker is the master ice carver here at the North Pole. We have the most beautiful sculptures all over town, and we have Spiniker to thank for many of them!

Polar bears haul gigantic blocks of ice to the display location, which is quite a sight to witness. The elves who carve the ice are also responsible for the care of these frosty beasts, treating them as pets, despite their enormous size.

Spiniker and his team create these winter works of art, and while they are not permanent structures, they do last a long time in our climate. Every year he comes up with a new theme for the sculptures. One year, each masterpiece represented a different North Pole sport—with Spiniker carving his favorite, Snow Dunk!

Snow Dunk is a little like golf. It's played on a ten-hole course where we toss spheres the size of large snowballs down a long fairway, rolling them into holes in the target zone. Spiniker is one of our best players, probably because he has been playing for most of his 438 years. He's been trying to help me for all 317 years that he's been on the council! He's trying his best to help improve my Snow Dunk skills, though I am admittedly a hopeless case.

Spiniker's efforts show others that patience is important and that we should share the skills we've mastered with anyone still learning.

GILSUM HOLLY

You must meet a very popular elf–our head clothing designer, Gilsum! She is admired for her fashion sense, but also because even at 402 years of age, she never takes herself too seriously. She designs clothing for all sorts of purposes, from work uniforms and athletic wear, to exciting formal outfits for me and Mrs. Claus to wear at the Snow Ball on New Year's Eve. She sure brings a lot of sparkle to our lives!

Gilsum also created my Christmas Eve ensemble, which is not only handsome (says Mrs. Claus), but keeps me toasty warm all night as I crisscross the globe delivering toys.

Another way Gilsum shares her flair is by decorating snowmen. It's considered a great honor if you find your creation accessorized by Gilsum. I remember one year when Mrs. Claus volunteered her time to build snowmen with a class of young elves at our school. The next day, the children were delighted to find that each one had been glamourized with sparkly ribbons, stylish hats, and glittery gloves.

Wherever you find Gilsum, you will also likely find two fluffy companions getting into mischief. They're her cats, Peaches (a white-and-orange tabby) and Shadow (a black Bombay). They love to play around in the fabrics at Gilsum's design room, but they never destroy her work. You can usually find them curled up and napping on their specially designed cat tree. They adore Gilsum as much as she adores them.

After 254 years on the council, Gilsum has convinced us all that the magic of fashion is to find your own style and let it sparkle with pride.

JERIX JINGLE

If anyone ever needs anything fixed, Jerix is the elf for the job. He's the head of our repair shop and runs a team of twenty-five talented technicians. All the elves on his team can maintain or fix most of the North Pole equipment, but when something more complicated comes up, Jerix is the elf that's called. He might be tinkering with a conveyor belt in the toy workshop one day, sorting out an irrigation problem at the greenhouses the next, and teaching apprentice elves the finer points of flying sleigh brakes after that. His skills earned him a place on the council 81 years ago.

When not up to his elbows in grease or wood glue, Jerix has two favorite pastimes. First, he loves to carve ornate wooden walking sticks. When Harvel harvests trees, he finds Jerix wonderful pieces of wood, and Jerix carves intricate designs into them before giving them to friends. There are many walking trails around the North Pole, and the ice can be tricky to navigate, so walking sticks are always appreciated for both their beauty and utility.

The second passion Jerix has is singing. That's why he started the Jingle Tones, a barbershop quartet! Jerix is the tenor of the group. At 434 years old, he's had many years to work on perfecting his smooth, melodic voice. You'll often hear him singing as he works on repairs or as he walks into a council meeting.

Jerix reminds us to live life with a song in our hearts, fix what needs fixing, and always walk tall.

BRINDLE CHEER

The North Pole is always a festive and beautiful place, and much of the credit goes to Brindle, our master gardener. Along with the thirty greenhouses managed by Mertin, we have twelve more that focus on flowers and plants. Brindle heads a team of sixty elves who plant, water, and maintain these luscious greenhouses.

At 687 years of age, Brindle has learned about plants from all around the world. She works hard to grow them at the North Pole and teach others about their unique qualities. (Her friend Silvien is actually the one who inspired her to share her knowledge with others!) Her most recent project is a program for young elves called Plant Magic for Minis. She works with the director of education to plan hands-on classes allowing school-age elves to learn about flowers and plants, including how to care for them.

Another special activity for Brindle involves poinsettias. She has three greenhouses dedicated specifically to growing these stunning symbols of the holiday season. Every year before Christmas, Brindle creates a giant display in city hall, using over two hundred plants in her design. It's always something completely different than the year before, and each display is more amazing than the last.

You wouldn't think Brindle has any extra time, but when she does, you'll often find her entertaining friends. When she hosts gatherings, along with delicious food and drinks there are always stunning floral displays on each table. On more than one occasion, Brindle has given Mrs. Claus one of these stunning arrangements, and it always brightens up our home.

In her 347 years on the council, Brindle has taught us to appreciate beauty from all around the world just as she cherishes the flowers she's discovered, cared for, and shared.

ELDIN PEPPERMINT

Now it's time to introduce you to the youngest member of the North Pole Council, Eldin. He's just eighty-four years old and has been on the council since he was thirty.

Eldin's story might have ended very differently, or perhaps not have started at all. You see, when he was born, Eldin almost didn't survive. He was in the hospital for many weeks, but I visited every day. Sometimes those who go through difficult circumstances end up being the strongest of us all, and I just knew Eldin was destined to be a very special elf.

Not only is Eldin the youngest member of the council, but he was the youngest elf ever to take on the job of director of education. As director, he strives to bring fun to all of his serious responsibilities. That's why he especially loves to be involved with the Northern Stars Tournament, an academic competition much like quiz bowl. In the Northern Stars Tournament, students earn places on teams and practice throughout the year for this weeklong event. Young elves enjoy studying hard to learn about many different topics, such as animals of the tundra, the physics of flying sleighs, and lyrics to Christmas carols.

Our philosophy at the North Pole is that we are lifelong learners. Elves are in the classroom from the age of six to twenty-two, followed by an apprenticeship, and Eldin works hard to make sure elves find the job that best suits their interests.

Eldin is a hard worker and very charming. He is incredibly smart, but more importantly, he goes out of his way to help others and make every elf smile. All of that, and he still has time to be a part of the Jingle Tones! He has a lovely bass voice that can soothe even the crankiest polar bear.

Eldin's actions remind us that hard work can also be fun and that we should always make a point to be kind to others.

AURORA MAHINA

Perhaps with a name like Aurora, this next elf was destined for her role here at the North Pole. Aurora is the head of our meteorology department, keeping a close eye on the weather and the sky.

This job is especially important on Christmas Eve, but her talents are put to good use every day of the year. She has fourteen elves on her team who gather data, make predictions, and make sure the elves are safe and the toy factory can stay operational. It can get very cold up here, with frequent blizzards, so it's important we're not caught off guard by nasty weather.

Long before Christmas Eve, Aurora works overtime to make sure she knows exactly what the weather patterns will be when I'm delivering toys all around the world. There have been years when she's had to devise complex plans to navigate me around storms, all the while making sure I don't miss any deliveries. This great scientific work earned Aurora a place on the council 183 years ago.

When her head isn't in the clouds, her nose is deep in a book. Reading is her passion, and she has magnificent bookshelves in her home to store all her treasures. She is always willing to lend out books for other elves to enjoy. Aurora finds it a delightful challenge to pick out stories that she thinks her friends will love. When she finds the right one, she can hardly wait to hear back from them with a review!

Mrs. Claus is always excited to get a new book recommendation, but she also loves to try and surprise Aurora with books she hasn't read yet. This can be delightfully difficult since Aurora has been reading for most of her 296 years!

Aurora has taught us to face challenges head-on as she demonstrates her courage by remaining calm during the most monstrous blizzards.

DECEMBER 12:
ORNIKA CANDYCANE

While I am the "big man in charge" of Christmas, the North Pole has its own leader—the mayor! For the past five years, Ornika has been the mayor of the North Pole.

Earning this position is quite an honor. Every citizen of the North Pole gets to select one elf in a secret nomination process. I then have the difficult task of selecting the deserving elf to serve as mayor of the North Pole. This job has been less difficult with Ornika, though, because for the past five years every single elf picked him for the job. Every single one! This just goes to show what an amazing job Ornika is doing and how respected he is.

Ornika has an infectious smile and absolutely exudes cheer. He visits places like toy workshops and schools to help the elves remember why our work is so important. In short—Ornika exemplifies the magic of Christmas!

Despite his important work, Ornika is humble and doesn't really like to be the center of attention. But he *does* love to participate in big celebrations. During the New Year's festivities, he loves riding in an ornate sleigh pulled by polar bears. The polar bears love it, too, because he always has fish biscuits in his pockets to reward the friendly beasts for all their hard work. It's not unusual to find a fluffy white cub trailing the mayor around town in hopes of an ear scratch and a treat.

Ornika also has other little ways to make a big impact. Elf houses are each unique in design and a great source of pride for their owners, and Ornika will create special decorations to secretly add to homes. He's very good about keeping the secret so the elves can discover the addition for a happy surprise!

At 527 years of age, Ornika has never let the magic of Christmas dim within himself, and he makes sure to keep it glowing strong in everyone around him too. Ornika shows us how easy it can be to earn respect when you celebrate the importance of others and enjoy the magic of life.

FAIRALY MISTLETOE

Young and ambitious are the words I would use to describe Fairaly, the head of the North Pole wrapping department. At just 142 years of age, she has certainly worked her way up from when she first entered the department. Fairaly started as an apprentice elf where she learned the art of tying bows. After much hard work, she eventually became a shift supervisor where she encouraged others to learn new skills. Now she is running the entire department!

Where Fairaly shines is helping her staff have fun while they work, creating contests and rewarding their efforts. She's inspired many other department heads with her creativity. Every time I visit the warehouse, it looks different because her team is always coming up with new themes and decorations. It keeps things fresh and new, and everyone takes pride in helping design and decorate the space.

While she loves crafting handmade bows, Fairaly has another artistic passion—drawing and painting. She's become so talented that sometimes her work is used to illustrate children's books that are created at the North Pole and delivered by me to children all over the world!

Fairaly is often inspired by the birds Silvien attracts to her feeders. The two nature-loving friends will sit and gaze out of the big bay windows at the feeders, Fairaly with her sketchbook and Silvien arranging flowers, both creating their next masterpiece. After working for a while on their art, the two friends will take a break and invite a couple other elves over to play their favorite card game, Santa's Secret Stash. It's a popular game all over the North Pole, and elves learn to play it when they are young. Maybe you will get to play it one day!

Even after just thirty-two years on the council, Fairaly has taught us all to have fun while we work hard and to strive toward ever-greater heights.

DECEMBER 14:

VICOLE CHRISBOCKLE

Everyone has heard about our talented reindeer, but let me introduce you to Vicole, the master of the stables.

At 437 years of age, Vicole has had a lot of time to study the reindeer and find the best ways to care for them. He has fifteen elves working with him who help to feed and train our special friends. Aside from the big night, there are two other very exciting events that highlight his team's work.

First, there is the Snow Ball Parade. This event happens every year on June 24th, and all the various departments in the North Pole create their own special floats that are led by the reindeer. Mrs. Claus and I signal the end of the parade as we ride by in my Christmas sleigh pulled by the previous year's team. That's right—each year a new team of reindeer flies me through the sky to deliver gifts.

This takes me to our second big reindeer event, the Reindeer Games. We actually have over fifty reindeer in our herd, and they train and compete for the honor of flying on Christmas Eve. The famous team from the song "Rudolph the Red-Nosed Reindeer" has actually only flown together fifty-seven times. That's not too many considering I've made the flight for hundreds of years!

During the event, the reindeer compete in twenty games. Vicole and his team give their all to make sure these majestic animals enjoy themselves and are ready to do their best. Vicole works hard to find just the right mix of green veggies, sweet fruits, and vitamins to keep the reindeer healthy and strong. Of course, they get treats sometimes too. Vicole will even share a bit of his favorite candy, Tinselflocks, with them. He has always felt most relaxed and comfortable when he is around the animals, and they love him in return.

Throughout his eighty-five years on the council, members have always understood that while Vicole is rather quiet around the other elves, he is respected for how he inspires others to be kind to animals.

BELTEEN CAROLS

I hope that you will be lucky enough to have an inspirational teacher like Belteen at some point in your life. She was a teacher at the North Pole school for many of her 397 years, and she recently became the headmistress.

It's hard to believe Belteen has time to be on the council with all she does for the school, but she has been an excellent contributor to the council for twenty-three years. At school, Belteen is very strict, but also much loved by all of the young elves. She brings that combination to her work in the council, too, making sure that we stay on track to get things accomplished. Belteen is dedicated to all of her students, investing in their futures and helping every elf reach their full potential.

One way she connects with the students and teachers is by giving out special flower notes. After writing an encouraging word or two—giving suggestions for ways to be challenged or recognizing a special accomplishment—she will fold the note into a flower and deliver it herself.

Along with paper folding, Belteen loves to knit. She creates scarves, capes, and blankets that are perfect for keeping warm in this frozen land. I wear one of her beautiful scarves when I fly around the world, and it keeps me warm even in the sharpest of winds.

Through her work on the council, Belteen reminds us that the best way to keep everyone motivated is by recognizing hard work with encouraging words.

PIPPLE CODERKNOCKS

Pipple is a strong elf at 529 years old—and he needs to be with his big job! Pipple is the head of the North Pole Grounds and Parks.

You might not realize just how big the North Pole is and how many places the NPGP crew is responsible for maintaining. There are twelve parks, all with trails that connect one to another. The team is also in charge of snow removal from the city streets and sidewalks—and the North Pole gets a whole lot of snow! The North Pole is always humming with activity, and we can't afford to be slowed down by not being able to get around. Pipple makes sure even the nastiest blizzard won't stop us.

With all of Pipple's expertise with snow, it won't surprise you that he is also very talented at carving snow sculptures. He's part of a club that creates beautiful works of snow art around the North Pole. During the winter festival, his club hosts a contest for elves to show off their creative carvings. While Pipple's team has yet to win, they typically place very high in the standings. My favorite entry was from the year they took second place with a sculpture of me in a bathtub filled with bubbles, holding a huge mug of hot cocoa topped with a swirly glob of whipped cream!

Pipple was invited to be a part of the council 217 years ago because he really understands the ins and outs of all of the spaces that make up the North Pole. He knows how to keep things running smoothly, especially when things get tough.

The council is grateful to Pipple for helping us remember that winning is not always the most important thing, as long as we're putting forth our best efforts and bringing joy to others.

-

DECEMBER 17:

GERRON GINGERBREAD

Today I would like to introduce you to Gerron, a very calm and levelheaded elf who has been on the council for 310 years. Gerron is an elf who can be relied on, so that's why she supervises the Naughty-and-Nice List. Her team of forty-two elves works in the field collecting data on the behavior of children around the world. Gerron gets especially excited when she sees a report about a child sharing the magic of Christmas, just like her friends on the council do!

Managing this list takes a lot of organization. It's important for Gerron to recognize the difference between mistakes and truly naughty choices. Of course that makes my job all the more challenging on the big night since there are so many children to visit, but I would never complain. Gerron also keeps track of who still believes in me. But don't worry—I still believe in you, even if you've stopped believing in me!

All that responsibility means that it's important for Gerron to take breaks and relax. That's when she takes to the snow for some cross-country skiing! As a youth she was a great racer, but now at 632 years old, she just enjoys getting out for the exercise.

Gerron also loves to sing, although she is a bit shy about singing in front of others. The perfect solution was for her to join the Elf Choir and Caroling group. Now she can sing her heart out while surrounded by supportive friends who love Christmas carols as much as she does. One day, when she's gained enough confidence, she might even start her own small group of all-female singers to perform alongside the Jingle Tones.

Gerron reminds us to always look for the *nice* in people, and to learn to forgive the *naughty!*

EMERICK SNOWBALL

I'd like to tell you about a real prankster named Emerick. He's one of our toy designers and has been on the council for fifty-two years. He was thrilled to be asked to join at his 200th birthday party! He's always trying to trick me with one stunt or another and is the best at finding a way to make me laugh. I chuckled for days the time he put a two-way radio in a teddy bear in my office. I had several great conversations with that bear before I figured out I was really talking to Emerick!

Emerick specializes in toys made out of wood. He's created some of our best model airplanes, but he especially loves dreaming up puzzle toys. His amazing workshop is filled with every random piece and part you could imagine. It's very well organized, and he knows just where to find everything he needs.

Whenever Emerick creates a new toy, he will invite his friends over to test it out so it can be perfected before he shares it with me. He takes great personal pride in making toys he knows will light up faces with smiles.

Emerick is a big kid at heart, and not only likes to play his own games, but many other elf games too. He's especially skilled at Patchwork Ball, which is similar to lacrosse. In this game, players use sticks with nets on one end to try to get yarn-like balls down a field and into one of five goals, each guarded by a goalie. The name of the game comes from the squares on the field that determine the boundary lines for players.

Even though Emerick loves his job and works hard, he knows not to take himself too seriously. He reminds the council of this lesson with every prank he pulls, and we love him for that.

FUZZEL TINDERPINE

Perhaps the best job in the North Pole belongs to Fuzzel. She is the head of festivals and entertainment, which means she plans all the wonderful events we enjoy up here at the North Pole. She and her team are bursting with ideas and always manage to pull off miracles. They decide (with great excitement!) the new theme for the Snow Ball Parade and the Great Summer Sleigh Ride Sing-Off. The crowning glory each year is the New Year's Eve Snow Ball, where we all celebrate the successful end to another Christmas season.

As part of her work with all the festivals, Fuzzel creates a wonderful assortment of collectable pins. The elves can hardly wait to see the designs for each event. These pins are given to those who show pureness of heart, and the elves wear them like badges of honor to show all the good they've done. At 314 years of age, Fuzzel understands the importance of recognizing good deeds and acts of kindness.

Fuzzel was selected to be on the council because she's levelheaded and hardworking, as well as very energetic and willing to help out others. She brings out the best in her fellow elves by being an excellent example.

No matter how large the event or how much there is to accomplish, Fuzzel does not let stress overwhelm her. She stays cool and calm—in part because she knows how to ask for help and trusts others to do their part.

There's a lot of hard work that gets accomplished at the North Pole, and Fuzzel teaches us the importance of sharing the workload so everyone has time to relax and enjoy the fun.

HABERTIN TWINKLE

The elves work very hard throughout the year to create the magic of Christmas, so it's important they have some vacation time! Habertin plays a special role in making this happen since he runs SNOW: Spectacular Northern Oasis World. SNOW is a wonderful wintery world of fun and games with a beautiful lodge that sits at the edge of the North Pole. For most of his 198 years, Habertin has been involved with running the resort, which has been passed down through his family for generations. His father taught him so much about how to run the business, especially about how to create a warm and relaxing environment.

Habertin is always dreaming up new forms of entertainment for his guests. There are several ice rinks where guests play games such as Pom-Pom Pull Away and Crack-the-Whip. He also helps organize skating races and ice tag, and some elves even enjoy ice dancing.

Other parts of the resort are set up for building snow forts and igloos. There are outdoor seating areas at various locations where you can sit and sip candy-cane cocoa in front of a blazing fire, delivered by elves on skis!

Spending time at SNOW is great fun, but one of my favorite parts of the resort is the twisting and turning toboggan trails that take you through forests and glowing ice tunnels. They even pass the animal sanctuary areas that protect local arctic foxes, moose, snowshoe hares, and other furry friends.

Even though he works very hard, Habertin takes time to enjoy all the fun at the resort, another important lesson he learned from his father. Habertin is the third generation in his family to be on the council. His father held the position until just five years ago when he retired to spend more time at SNOW, just as his father had done many years ago. We have seen firsthand how much can be passed from one generation to the next as we watch Habertin thrive in his roles as both the head of the resort and a council member.

Habertin reminds us how much can be passed down from one generation to the next and how important it is to learn from your family.

GABERDIEN SPRINKLES

I am sure that you've been wondering about which elf is in charge of all the letters that get sent to the North Pole. Her name is Gaberdien and her responsibilities are enormous! After all, we wouldn't want to let down any of our friends who believe in the magic of Christmas. Gaberdien truly understands and appreciates all the love you put into the notes you write to me.

Gaberdien's team works in the Snow Globe building. The technology in this building is constantly being updated, and Gaberdien's team uses all of the latest techniques to keep track of requests from all over the world. The latest scanning system allows me to view all the letters on my personal Ice-pad.

It's important that the head of this department is organized and meticulous about details, which is why Gaberdien is a perfect fit. In case any elf might think she's too serious, one only has to hear Gaberdien's melodious giggle to know she likes to have fun. It's quite infectious and makes others want to laugh too! Whether she's playing games with friends or baking Christmas cookies, whatever room she's in is always filled with joy.

Christmas cookies are her favorite food, but don't bother asking what type is her favorite—because she can never decide! We love to sit and chat after Christmas so I can tell her all about the new varieties I've tried along the journey. So it's no surprise that she's in charge of the Christmas cookie exchange at the North Pole. It certainly takes someone with her organizational skills to keep track of all the elves who want to participate.

After 271 years of being on the council, Gaberdien has helped us all see that we should embrace new things and live life with a giggle.

BIXTON CHESTNUT

I wish with all my heart that the magic of Christmas could be strong enough to protect us from the dangers of the world, but there are forces that threaten even our joyful existence. That's why we have been especially glad to have Bixton as part of our council for the past 210 years. He is the head of security and takes his job very seriously.

Bixton needs to maintain the security web that keeps our North Pole community hidden and safe. It's an interesting combination of magic and technology that is ever-changing and requires him to constantly learn new techniques and create updated programs. You will never see Bixton without his special friend, Yuki the snowy owl. Not only is he a wonderful companion, but Yuki helps Bixton with his security by giving him eyes in the sky.

Bixton is always keeping watch for the Humbugs, a group of creatures who have lost hope. They are always trying to think of ways to interrupt the magic of Christmas because they have forgotten it can bring joy and peace to the world.

Bixton likes to stay strong of mind and also in body. Everything he does comes back to helping him better keep us safe. To keep his body strong, he loves to go out to the ice cliffs and climb. One of his favorite things is to sit at great heights and watch the northern lights illuminate the sky. He also likes to find caves, and will often disappear for hours as he explores. I think that Bixton enjoys the solitude of these activities. He has so much to keep track of, and so many people that he is responsible for keeping safe, that he sometimes needs time on his own.

Many find happiness in spending a lot of time together, singing and decorating, and having parties. It's good to be reminded by Bixton that some elves need alone time to be at their best when working to create and protect the magic of Christmas.

DECEMBER 23:
ABERDEEN MITTENFOLLY

You must meet our spunky keeper of the books, Aberdeen! She is a youthful 357 years old and has spent many of those years creating the spectacular library at the North Pole.

The North Pole library is filled with light and energy and magic. Every book that has ever been imagined about Christmas, including this one, can be found floating and dancing its way around the room. You don't even need to find the title in a catalogue. Just think of the book in your mind and you will soon find it floating into your hands!

Aberdeen has worked hard to acquire every book that children have ever requested in their letters to me. She also likes to pay special attention to collecting books that teach us about the world. Most elves don't get to spend time outside of the North Pole, but they want to know everything they can about other places, people, and traditions. So Aberdeen stocks books about animals in Australia, clothing in Cambodia, food in France, and so much more.

You can walk into the library at any time and stumble across wonderful discussions about this book or that book. There's even a magical room that allows the books to come to life so we can interact with the stories.

Aberdeen's favorite pastime outside of the library is downhill skiing. We have an outstanding ski resort on the far side of the North Pole with six picturesque runs that trail through forests and offer wonderful views of our frozen world. On the lower portion of the resort there is a run with marvelous Candy Cane trees and garlands of evergreen with sparkling lights, making nighttime magical and fun.

Aberdeen brings her excitement about the world to the council. She reminds us to embrace creativity and imagination, just like the authors of the books in the library.

BAXTER PARCELS

Even though Christmas Eve is obviously my busiest night, the North Pole is at work all year round making toys. All of those toys need a place to be stored, and Baxter is in charge of that task as the warehouse supervisor.

In his 174 years, Baxter has become very strong, mostly from all of his hard work lifting and moving packages. The warehouse has become high-tech and takes advantage of some cool new machines, but Baxter still needs to be very physically fit to do his job.

All year, toys are made and stored as they are readied for children all around the world. Once a toy request comes through on my Ice-pad, the gift is wrapped and sorted, ready to be packed into my magical bag.

Baxter is fair, and no matter how stressful the day, he always keeps his cool. That is why his team respects him so much, and why he was invited to join the council twenty-four years ago.

I'm also excited to tell you about Baxter's interesting home. He was the first resident of The Groves, a community of tree houses. The houses are built right into a gigantic tree system with four sturdy trunks that grow out of one strong base. They often have intricately carved staircases that twist and turn around the structures. The homes are a wonderful combination of art and comfort, and they are designed by the owners and built cooperatively by all the neighbors.

When Baxter isn't sorting gifts or helping to build new homes in The Groves, you can likely find him on an outdoor adventure at a wilderness park with his friends. With how hard he works indoors at the warehouse, he likes to spend his free time out in nature.

Whether in the warehouse or building homes at The Groves, Baxter demonstrates a keen sense of how to get people to work together. The council has learned from him that these important behind-the-scenes details are what truly make magic happen.

DECEMBER 25:

CHRISTMAS MORNING

The big day has finally arrived, and I hope your morning was magical! I had a delightful time visiting homes all around the world, snacking on Christmas cookies, and admiring decorations. I hope you've enjoyed meeting all the elves on the council. We will continue to work hard throughout the upcoming year to keep the magic of Christmas alive.

You can help the North Pole Council by remembering all the special skills and talents of the elves you met and doing your best to keep those lessons going all year long. Bake and share a special treat with friends and family. Find the beauty in the natural world around you. Work together with others to make things easier. Work hard while still finding time to relax and have fun! The magic of Christmas can last all year with your help.

Up at the North Pole, we'll be taking just a little time off to recover from all the hard work, but then we'll celebrate at the Snow Ball on New Year's Eve. Then we'll get right back to designing new toys, training all the reindeer, teaching our young elves about the magic of Christmas, and so much more.

Now, if you'll excuse me, I'm going to relax in my chair by the fire with a steaming cup of cocoa. I want to tell Mrs. Claus about the wonderful places I visited last night. It is likely, however, that I will drift off to sleep before I get too far into sharing about my fantastic journey. I'm sure that the smell of Belina's freshly baked cinnamon rolls will wake me up after a short nap, and then I'll finish regaling Mrs. Claus with my tales. Maybe I'll even tell her about your home!

Celebrate and enjoy today with your loved ones. We'll be back next year with more love and fun as we share the magic of Christmas.

Merry Christmas to all,

Santa Claus

Have a loved one help you write one good deed you did every day in December.

Now make your own calendar and keep the magic of Christmas going all year long!

A NOTE FROM THE CREATOR

When you take time to think of ways to spread kindness and help others, you are creating the magic of Christmas.

My favorite thing about the holiday season is seeing people go out of their way to make others smile. It can be so simple! Giving out compliments, wishing strangers "Happy holidays," or even saying *please* and *thank you*. My grandma always told me that *please* and *thank you* can be more powerful than you think. While Christmas presents are great, it doesn't cost anything to be kind.

So spread cheer! There are so many ways to brighten someone's day.

Focus on creating the holiday spirit for others and you'll feel the magic of Christmas all year.

Rob Sutherland

ACKNOWLEDGMENTS

*Just like Christmas wouldn't be Christmas without Mrs. Claus,
there are a lot of people who helped bring this book to life . . .*

Thank you to:

Will Sutherland
Barb Sutherland
Maddie Krusmark
Christopher Teipner
Kelsey Zieman
Kelsey Freundschuh
Lisa Ferland
JC Lippold
Tom Emig
The Clark family
Jennifer Priester
The Julson family
Maxwell Freudenthal
The Forsberg family
Brian Cern
Mark Olson
The Westrup family
The Ringsdore family
Dean Elwell
The Bresette family
The Luchsinger family
The Van Ranst family
The McNamara family
The Burke family
Warren Sampson
Kristen Heeringa
The Hannula family
The MacRae family
Anna Rose Meeds

Ella Sutherland
Jill Krusmark
Gavin Krusmark
Kyle Schwartz
Amy Bearth
Angela Dawson
The Bannwarth family
Kristen Kruegel
Garrette Wertz
Alyssa Soukup
The Tatarka family
The Pearson family
The Lodahl family
Timm Holmly
The Dunn family
Krysti Bink
The Lampert family
The Pietig family
Deb Sherman
The Bark family
The Yarusso family
The Tonrey family
The Sharratt family
The Eklund family
The Wallace family
The Quarter Group
Melissa Faust
The Corbett family

Matthew Sutherland
Cary Krusmark
Peg Sutherland
Chad Garrels
The Bartkey family
The Hestwood family
The Monk family
Ryan DeLaCroix
Jennifer Meister
Barry Anderson
Sue Kuta
The Livingston family
The Wellens family
Amy Krattley
Emily Tinawi
Barb Petersen
The Roettger family
Heather Market-Sullivan
Dan and Debbie Market
The Freundschuh family
The Turino family
Teresa Dahlem
Susan Cathey
Jeff Musch
Bob and Anne Sutherland
Carolynne Thomas
Joe, Joy, and Jenny Johnson
Matt Wayne

And all our family members and friends who have been so supportive!

ABOUT THE CREATOR

Rob Sutherland is the artistic director and co-founder of Ashland Productions, a youth-mentoring theater in Maplewood, Minnesota. Rob has been a part of many theatrical productions, but his favorite role is dad to his three beautiful, amazing, and talented children, Will, Ella, and Matthew. Rob has a bachelor's degree in marketing education from UW-Stout. Rob has enjoyed bringing this project to life (with the help of this amazing team!) because he loves the season of Christmas. He hopes this book will become a tradition that brings joy and spreads the magic of Christmas.

ABOUT THE WRITER

Rachel Cathey is a teacher in Minnesota, where she lives with her son and a small zoo of pets. When she is not writing, she enjoys acting with a variety of community theatres and directing youth productions. Rachel is thrilled to be part of a team that's sharing the magic of Christmas through the North Pole Council, as holidays and family traditions have always been an important part of her life.

ABOUT THE ILLUSTRATORS

Jacqui Davis was born in Johannesburg, South Africa, and moved to the United Kingdom as a kid. She currently lives and works in Lytham-St-Annes, which is great for walks through the woods or ambles along the estuary. After graduating in animation from Staffordshire University, Jacqui began freelancing. She enjoys painting everything from adorable animals to villainous wizards, and has always been passionate about bringing life to characters in her work. When she's not painting she enjoys keeping the creative mojo going by doing a spot of writing.

Josiah Hendrickson is happy to be on the 24 Elves creative team. He was inspired to work on this project to give kids moments with their families and friends that focus on the higher values of life. It's Josiah's hope that these elves and their good deeds present children and parents with an opportunity to discuss those warm lessons money could never hope to buy.

Follow the North Pole council
with a parent or guardian
at www.24elves.com
and on Facebook @24elves.